T0380969

In Search of
a Big Patch of Grass

Written by **Joy Mal**

Illustrated by Dwight Nacaytuna and Billy-J Wolnicki

To order additional copies of this book, contact:
Xlibris
1-800-455-039
www.xlibris.com.au
Orders@Xlibris.com.au

Illustrated by Dwight Nacaytuna and Billy-J Wolnicki

ISBN: Softcover   978-1-7960-0588-2
        Hardcover   978-1-7960-0589-9
        EBook   978-1-7960-0587-5

Print information available on the last page

Rev. date: 08/31/2019

To my children, Matt, Jessi, Billy-J, and Abi, and to their children.

A special thanks to Billy-J, for contribution of her illustrative work.

All grown-ups were once children... but only few of them remember it.
Antoine de Saint Exupêry, *The Little Prince*

My mum was a child once, just like me. When she was little,
she lived in a flat in a big city.

Near her flat was a small patch of grass with a little sign poked into it. The sign read: "KEEP OFF THE GRASS!"

On the way home from church, wearing her good Sunday's shoes, Mum would walk pathways of a big, green park. The park had fancy steps and historical statues, amazing fountains, and lots of beautiful trees and flowers. She would love to climb the trees, run her fingers over their bark, smell them up close. She dreamed about running across perfectly trimmed, luscious grass barefooted, feeling its texture between her toes, and wriggling her fingers in the cool water of the park's biggest fountain. But she was not allowed. The park had its rules. She could only observe, restricted to the grey, concrete pathways. No touching!

Even though the park was very beautiful to walk through and fun to look at, my mum felt that she didn't belong there. She was only passing through.

Every summer, Mum would go by train to visit her grandparents. They lived in the last house at the end of a small village. They kept horses, cows, pigs, ducks, chickens, and sheep.

Each morning, all the village children would gather the sheep and lead them to the pasture. They would stop at Mum's grandparents gate. Mum couldn't wait to join them!

The fields were green, peaceful, and endless. The children wore no shoes. They laughed as the grass tickled their toes. They could run their fingers through its different textures and feel its warmth. They walked. They run. They felt connected and whole. They belonged.

While the sheep were feeding, Mum played in puddles, catching tadpoles and froglets with the other children, wriggling her fingers in the cool water. They played houses and shops. They built castles and made wreaths of wild flowers. They were kings and queens.

When summer ended, Mum would go back to the big city

... to the flat near the small patch of grass with the little sign poked into it: "KEEP OFF THE GRASS!"

As the years passed, her desire to walk the park faded away. She was growing older.

When she thought she was old enough, Mum married my dad and thought about having children of her own.

Then hard times came. There were food shortages, and Mum stood in long lines, using food stamps* to buy meat, sugar, chocolate, and other things they needed. Tanks filled the city streets, and the secret police watched everyone day and night.

Mum fled, moving houses and countries

... in search of a big patch of grass.

Now, my mum sits in a bay window, watching her own children play. She rests.

Our garden is big and green, and behind it are flowing fields of grass. It looks endless to us. We play houses and shops, build castles, and make wreaths of wild flowers.

We explore garden puddles, catching tadpoles and froglets, wriggling our fingers in the cool water.

We never wear shoes.

We laugh when grass tickles our toes. We run our fingers through its different textures and feel its warmth. We walk. We run. We feel connected and whole. We belong.

We are kings and queens in an endless, peaceful field, where all things are possible.

* Food stamps or ration stamps - issued by a government to allow the holder to obtain food or other commodities that are in short supply during wartime or in other emergency situations. A person could not buy a rationed items without also giving the grocer the right ration stamp.

In Poland during the Communist era, food stamps were given out monthly with an employee's pay. The foods rationed included: flour, candy, chocolates, detergent, cigarettes, alcohol, soap, oil/lard, meat (all by grams/packs/bottles), and milk (by liters). Other items were available for purchasing with cash but they were hard to find.

Joy Mal was born in Warsaw, Poland, where she published several poems and short stories before migrating to Australia in 1982. Now residing in Queensland, she works as a psychiatric nurse balancing this often-challenging work with practices of self-care and gratitude. She finds joy by investing in lives of younger generations, something she explores in her book *In Search of a Big Patch of Grass*. Joy is also engaged with the Therapeutic Writing Institute, Colorado, United States, where she discovered 'Writing for Healing', which she implements in both her work as a psychiatric nurse and her day-to-day life. Joy is a member of Queensland Writers Centre in Australia.

Printed in the United States
By Bookmasters